TIES TO THE PAST
The Poles

Tana Reiff

A Pacemaker® **HOPES** *and* **DREAMS 2** Book

FEARON/JANUS/QUERCUS
Belmont, California

Simon & Schuster Supplementary Education Group

HOPES *and* DREAMS 2

Cover photo: Tony Freeman/PhotoEdit
Cover Design: Rucker Huggins
Illustration: Duane Bibby

ISBN 0–8224–3803–8
Library of Congress Catalog Card Number: 92–71066

Printed in the United States of America
1. 9 8 7 6 5 4 3 2
MA

CONTENTS

1 Planning a Family

Buffalo, New York, 1900

Stanislaus and Zofia Koloski
came to America
by ship from Poland.
Their trip to America
was long and hard.
When they got
to Ellis Island
they had no idea
where they would go.
They only knew
that they were in New York.
So when the other Poles
got in line
to buy train tickets,
Stan and Zofia
stepped in behind them.

Someone said
there were jobs
in Buffalo, New York.

There was also a church there
called St. Stanislaus.
Stan Koloski said
he wanted to live
where there was a church
named after his saint.
So Buffalo is where
Stan and Zofia went.

Thousands of Poles
had come to Buffalo
before the Koloskis.
Many were young men
who came alone
to make some money.
Many were young married people
like Stan and Zofia.
Almost all the Poles
came from farm areas.·
Living in a city
would be new and strange.

"Doesn't matter
if you can't speak English,"
a Polish neighbor told Stan.
"Go down to the train station.

They will give you work.
They only care
if you have a strong body."

   "I have no money,"
said Stan.
"I speak no English.
But a strong body
I do have!"
He pushed out his chest
to show his neighbor.
"See this?
I can lift my wife
with one arm!"
He lifted Zofia
off the ground.
Zofia let out
a high little scream.

   Stan found work
at the main train station.
He worked 12-hour days.
His job
was to load boxes
onto train cars.
A weak man

could never have done
Stan's job.

The work was hard.
But Stan made friends
with other Poles.
And he looked forward
to a hot meal
with Zofia
at the end of every day.

"It's time
to have some children,"
he told Zofia
at dinner one night.
"I want
a big family."

"I will be glad
to have children around,"
said Zofia.
She smiled at her husband.
Now that Stan had a job,
she too wanted children.
They talked about this
all during dinner.

Then, as Stan
was cleaning his plate
with his bread,
he said,
"Now I must go
to my meeting."

"What meeting?"
Zofia asked.

"Some Poles in Buffalo
have started a group,"
Stan explained.
"This group will work
for the Polish people.
My Polish friends
asked me to come along."

Stan stood up
and gave his wife
a big hug.
Then off he went
to his meeting.

Thinking It Over

1. What groups do you know of that work for their own people?

2. What kinds of jobs do people take when they are new in the country?

3. How can you tell who runs things in the Koloski home?

2 Dom Polski

A man stood up
in front of the group.
He spoke in Polish.
Stan listened
to every word.

"We Poles in Buffalo
have problems,"
the man said.
"The new Poles
who come in
need help to find
a place to live."

Stan knew
this was true.
He and Zofia
lived in one room
of another family's house.
Most of the young men alone
lived in rooming houses.

"Some of us
need to learn English,"
the man in front went on.

Stan supposed
this was true, too.
His only English words
were "Yes," "No,"
and a few others
he needed at work.

"And we all need
a place to get together,"
said the man.
"We need a place
to dance and drink
and keep up our Polish life.
We need a Dom Polski—
a Polish home.
We must all work together
to raise enough money.
Then we will build
our Dom Polski!"

Stan couldn't wait
to join in on these ideas.

But first he and Zofia
had to move
into their own new home.
The rail company
built little houses
in the Polish East Side of town.
Because Stan worked
for the rail company,
he could buy
one of the houses
on Fillmore Street.
On weekends
he did some work
on the new place.
Zofia covered the windows.
She set up the kitchen.
She made the little house
into a real home.

Less than a year after
Stan and Zofia moved in,
their first son was born.
They named him Gregor.
He was a happy baby.
He never gave his parents
any trouble at all.

Then Stan and Zofia
were ready to help raise money
for Dom Polski.
Bricks for the building
were being sold
for a dollar each.
Stan and Zofia
bought five bricks.
Everyone in the group
had to pay a tax
to raise more money.
They bought some land
on Broadway,
on Buffalo's East Side.

By the summer of 1905,
it was time
to lay the cornerstone
of the new building.
The Polish people
in the area
planned a big day
around the cornerstone.
First they held a Mass
at their church
to thank God.

Then they marched
down the street.
The parade ended
where Dom Polski
was being built.
The priest
gave a speech.
He blessed the cornerstone.

One year later
Dom Polski opened its doors
to Polonia—
the Poles of Buffalo.
Everyone danced the polka
in the big room upstairs.
It was a day
that Stan and Zofia Koloski
would never forget.

Dom Polski
became a busy place.
Stan and Zofia went there
every Sunday after church.
They took turns
going to English classes
at Dom Polski.

They needed some English
to become U.S. citizens.

Zofia also enjoyed
the library at Dom Polski.
The walls were lined
with old Polish books.
Zofia had never seen
so many books,
not even in Poland.
When she had time,
she took Gregor along
to the library.
She would read
for an hour or two.
Then she would walk home
to Fillmore Street
and make Stan's dinner.

Thinking It Over

1. Have you ever helped
   to raise money for something?
   What did you do?

2. Would you be more interested
   in the library
   or the dance hall?
   Why?

3. What groups
   do you belong to?
   What is it
   that makes a group
   stick together?

3 Poland Needs Help!

The Koloskis' second child
was very different
from the first.
Gregor smiled all day.
Kassia, the new baby, cried.
As the children grew,
Gregor always did
as he was told.
Kassia had her own ideas
and a strong will.
Gregor made trucks
out of cans
and played little games.
Kass, as they called her,
never wanted to play along.
She would rather
look at the books
that Zofia brought home
from the library.

"How could we have
two children
so different from each other?"
Stan would ask Zofia.

Zofia had three more babies.
Each was different
from the one before.
But none of the children
was like Kass.
She had a mind of her own.

All five children
slept in one little room.
It was a lot of people
for the little house
on Fillmore Street.
But they all fit.
They even took in a boarder.
The family needed
every penny.

One night
Stan came home from work

with big news.
"The United States
has joined the war
over in Europe!"
he told the family.
"Now we can help
to free our dear Poland!"

Zofia had read
the Polish newspapers.
She knew all about
the Fatherland's problems.
A long time ago
Poland had been taken over
and split up between
Germany, Austria, and Russia.
Now that the United States
had joined the war
against Germany,
there might be a way
for Polish-Americans
to help the Fatherland.

"President Wilson
wants 100,000 men right away,"
said Stan.

He wished he could be
one of those men,
but he was too old.
"At Dom Polski
we will sign up men
to go to war,"
Stan went on.
"Gregor, you are
almost 16 years old.
You look old enough.
I want you
to be the first boy in line
to sign up."

"Of course, Father,"
said Gregor.
He hated the idea
of fighting in a war.
But he wanted
to help Poland.
Besides, he always did
what he was told.

"Zofia, you will join
the Red Cross,"
Stan told his wife.

"Yes, I will,"
said Zofia.
"I will do all I can
for dear Poland."

"I will buy
Liberty Bonds,"
said Stan.
"The United States needs
all the money
we can raise.
The Polish newspaper
says to buy until it hurts!"

"And you, Kass,
will leave school,"
said Stan.
"You will get a job.
It's time to do your part
for this family."

Thinking It Over

1. What does it mean
   to have a mind
   of one's own?

2. What would you do
   if you were told
   to leave school
   and get a job?

3. Have you ever
   believed strongly
   in a war?
   Why or why not?

4. How does each person
   in your family
   do his or her part?

4 A Mind of Her Own

"But Father—"
Kass began.
"I want to go on
to high school.
I want to finish school."

"School is a waste of time
for a girl,"
said Stan to his daughter.
"Your mother didn't go
to high school,
did you, Zofia?"

"No," said Zofia,
her head down.

"I wish
I could have finished school,"
she told Kass that night.
"But this is not
the way we Poles do things."

"I am American!"
Kass cried.
"This is America!
I have a school to go to.
I should use it.
I have the rest of my life
to work!"

"Take care
with the word *should*,"
said Zofia.
"You say
that you should go to school.
Your father says
that you should go to work.
Your *should*
is less important than
your father's *should*.
You must do
as your father says."

"I will die
if I can't go to school,"
said Kass.
"Please, please,
don't make me leave school."

"Your father
has the last word,"
said Zofia.

"How about if I work
and go to school?"
Kass asked.

"How can you do both?"
Zofia wondered.
"School and a job
both take a lot of time."

"Let me try,"
said Kass.

"Ask your father,"
said Zofia.

Kass told Stan
about her idea.

"You have always had
a mind of your own,"
said Stan.
"I don't know

where you got it.
I'll put it this way.
You bring home money
from a full-time job.
Don't worry about school.
You can't do both!"

"Please, Father!
I'll work *and* go to school!"
she cried.
"I'll make it all work!
You'll see."

"It won't work,"
said Stan.
A hard look
came over his face.
"And let me say this.
As things stand now,
you are not a member
of this family.
Any daughter of mine
listens to her father."

Kass could think of
nothing more to say.

She knew that she
had crossed her father.
A good Polish girl
would not do that.
She loved her father.
But she felt
that she must go to school.
She would have to find
the way back
into her father's heart.

Thinking It Over

1. Have you ever had
   a "falling out"
   with a member
   of your family?
   Did you work things out?
   How?

2. Do you have a job
   and go to school?
   How does this work out?

3. Should children
   always listen to their parents?
   Is there ever a time
   when it is OK
   not to listen to parents?

5 The First to Sign Up

Kass found a job
in a soap factory.
School let out at 3:00.
Kass wasted no time
as she walked ten blocks
to the factory.
She packed soap into boxes
until 11:00 at night.
Then she came home
and did her school work.
She went to bed
at 2:00 in the morning.
Five hours later
she was up again
and off to school.

Kass was now leading
such a busy life
that she didn't know
it was army sign-up day
at Dom Polski.

Her father was
up early that day.
He woke up Gregor.

"Out of bed, young man!"
Stan called to the boy.
"You're in the army now!"
He threw off Gregor's sheets.
He grabbed his son
by the hair.

Gregor rubbed his eyes
to wake up.
"This is the big day!"
were the first words
out of Gregor's mouth.

Kass woke up
when she heard
her father's voice.
She saw that it was
still dark outside.
She did not have to get up
for school just yet.
So she turned over
and went back to sleep.

But the three little children
woke up with Gregor.
"You three come along,"
said Stan.
"See your big brother
join the U.S. Army."

"I'll stay home,"
said Zofia.
"I'll have a hot lunch ready
when you get back.
You'll need it.
Have you seen the snow?"

Snow was nothing new
in Buffalo.
During the winter
it snowed two or three days
out of the week.
There was almost always
snow on the ground.
But during the night
there had been a big storm.
They called it a *lake snow*.
Lake snows were the worst.
This morning,

the snow blew around
and made mountains
against the houses.

Stan opened the front door.
Before him
was a wall of white.
Some snow fell
right into the house.

"Get the shovel!"
Stan called to Zofia.
He dug his way out.
Then he dug out a trail.
He walked in front.
Gregor and the three children
walked in a line behind him.

Dom Polski
was just around the corner.
But in the snow
it took a half hour
to get there.

Ten young men
were already in line.

Stan was angry.
"I wanted you
to be first,"
he said to Gregor.
"The snow made us late."

Stan walked up
to the head of the line.
"I'm going to put
my son Gregor
in front here,"
he told the first young man.
"He's going to Europe
to free our dear Poland."

"We all are going,"
said the young man,
who was really only a boy.
"But Gregor may go first."

Thinking It Over

1. Why do you think
   it was so important to Stan
   that Gregor be first in line?

2. What weather problems
   do you have to deal with
   where you live?

3. Would you work as hard as Kass
   just so you could stay in school?

6 The Polish Club

President Wilson's first call
was for 100,000 men.
He got what he asked for.
And 40,000 of them
were from Polish families.

Gregor left for Europe.
Zofia cried for days.
She too wanted
to help Poland.
She only wished
she could go to war
instead of her son.

Zofia also felt sad
because she saw so little
of Kassia.
The girl
was at school or work
most of the time.
She was home

only to sleep.
And once a week
she handed over
all the money she made
to her father.
He took every dollar
without a word
or a smile.

"Let her stop working,"
Zofia begged Stan.
"Can't you see
the girl is half dead?
This is too much for her.
She never gets
enough sleep."

"What good is a child
who doesn't help the family?"
Stan said.
"She can leave school
if she wants.
But not the job.
And you, Zofia,
would be better
not to cross me either."

It was the last time
Zofia raised a question
about Kass.
Stan's mind was set.

Stan didn't have time
to think much
about any of the children.
He was getting busy
with a new group.
The Polish Club
was working to get Poles
into high office.
"We must make sure
to take care of Poland,"
Stan said.
"The Germans and the Irish
are in office now.
They don't care
about Poland's interests.
Only we do."

"Why don't you
run for office yourself?"
Zofia asked him.

"I don't speak
good enough English,"
he told her.
"We are working
for a man named
Benek Popowski.
We want him
on the city council.
He will be a big man
in this city.
Next we will send him
to Washington!"

"And what about you?"
Zofia asked.

"I will be a big man
in the Polish Club,"
said Stan.

Every night
Stan was out
knocking on doors.
"Vote for Popowski!"
he told everyone.

When Popowski won,
there was a big party
at Dom Polski.
Stan and Zofia
and all their friends
danced the polka
until the sun came up.

Thinking It Over

1. Would you work
   to get someone
   into high office?
   What sort of person
   would that be?

2. Why is it important
   to vote?

3. Is there someone
   in your home
   who has "the last word"?

7 A Leader of Men

After Benek Popowski
won a seat
on the city council,
the Polish Club
needed a new cause.

About the same time,
the war in Europe ended.
Papers were signed.
A treaty
between Germany and Poland
had to be worked out.

"We should work
toward a good treaty
for the Fatherland,"
spoke Stan to the Polish Club.

"Leave that work
to the U.S. government,"
called out another man.

"Polish groups
in other cities
are putting the heat
on the U.S. government,"
said Stan.
"We must do this, too.
Take a vote tonight.
Let's see how we feel."

"Who thinks we should
stick only to our work
here in Buffalo?"
asked the man in front.

About half the hands
went up.

"Who thinks we should
work for a treaty
for the Fatherland?"
the man then asked.

The other half
of the hands went up.
Stan's hand
was one of them.

"Now what do we do?"
asked the man.
"Our group
is half and half."

Stan Koloski stood up.
"If you want to work
for a fair treaty,
come with me!
We will start
a new group
for this important work!"
He began to walk
out of the room.

"What are you doing?"
asked the man in front.
"There are already
enough Polish clubs.
We don't need another one."

But one by one,
men began to follow Stan.
About 25 men
followed Stan Koloski
out the door.

"You are strong men!"
Stan told his new group.
"We will see to it
that Poland is free,
once and for all!"

The new group
talked to people
in the U.S. government.
They wrote letters.
When Poland became free,
Stan Koloski felt sure
that he had helped
to make it happen.

Thinking It Over

1. What would you do
   if a group you were in
   began to have ideas
   different from your own?

2. How do you feel
   about making your voice heard
   by the government?

3. What kind of person
   do you think
   would be a good leader?

8 Leaving School

It was a happy day
when Gregor came home
from the war.
He came home
in one piece.
But he seemed different.
"You are not a boy now,"
Zofia told him.
"You have become a man."

Gregor had just turned 18.
He looked and acted
well past that age.

"What will you do next?"
Kass asked her brother.

"I've made up my mind
to become a priest,"
he said.
"Nothing would please

our parents more.
And what of you, Kass?
You don't look well.
Are you all right?"

"Oh, Gregor,"
she cried.
"What am I to do?
I feel so old and tired.
After school and work,
there is nothing left of me."

"Maybe you should
leave school,"
said Gregor.

Kass put her hands
over her ears.
"I don't want to hear that!"
she cried.

"You must face facts,"
said Gregor in a kind voice.
"You can't do everything."

"And Papa still
does not speak to me,"
said Kass.
"I sleep here
under the same roof.
But I am not
a member of the family.
Perhaps you are right.
Perhaps to leave school
is the only way I can live."

The next morning
Kass went to see
Sister Mary Halina,
the head of the school.
Kass was crying
as she sat down
by Sister Mary Halina's desk.
"I must leave school,"
Kass told her.

"I am sorry,"
said Sister Mary Halina.
"God be with you, child.

May your life's work
make your place in heaven."

The next morning
Kass's hands shook.
She told her father
that she had left school.
She waited to hear him say,
"You are my child again."

But Stan did not
say those words.
Instead, he said,
"It is too late.
You already crossed me.
You must do
much more than leave school
to be a member
of this family again."

"But Father—"
Kass began,
as she had done
when her father

first told her
to leave school.

   "You become
a true Polish girl,"
said Stan.
"You show some interest
in the Fatherland.
You show me
a happy face
as you dance the polka
in a bright-colored dress.
You speak Polish
in this house.
You show me that you
are a true member
of this family.
Then I will know
that you really are Polish."

   While Stan spoke to her,
Kass was getting angry.
"Why does he always
think he's right

about everything?"
she asked herself.

Kass turned
and headed for the door.
She wished she could
walk out of the house
and just keep going.
But where could she go?
What could she do?
She knew it was
out of the question.

Kass stood by the door.
She was still thinking about
what her father had just said.
It was true.
She had little interest
in Polish things.
She saw herself
as an American
with Polish parents.
Then she turned her face
back toward her father.

"If you
miss the past so much,
you should go back
to Poland!"
she screamed.
Hearing herself
say that to her father
surprised even Kass.

Thinking It Over

1. Do you think
   that Stan is being fair
   to his daughter
   to ask these things of her?

2. Do you think
   a person new to a country
   should stick only to the old ways?
   Why or why not?

3. How can it be good
   for a person
   to stick with the ways
   of the old country?

9 Two Young Americans

Kass met Edward
at the soap factory.
He had just come
from Poland.
He lived
in a rooming house
just down the street
from the Koloskis' house.

Edward wanted nothing more
than to be American.
He changed the way
he spelled his first name.
Eduard became *Edward*.
He even made
his last name short
so it didn't sound Polish.
He changed
Warnovitski to *Warner*.
His hair was cut
like an American's.

He spent much of his money
on American clothes.
He went to English classes
at Dom Polski.

Edward showed interest
in Kassia Koloski
because she wasn't like
some other Polish girls.
She seemed
more like an American girl.

Kass and Edward
began to see each other
almost every night.
Stan didn't seem to care
that Kass was out so often.
After all,
he didn't see her
as a member of his family.

"You are the best thing
that ever happened to me,"
Kass told Edward one night.

"I feel the same
about you, Kass,"
said Edward.
"Will you be my wife?
I will soon become
a real American.
We will save our money.
Then we will buy a house
outside of the city.
Wouldn't that be grand?"

"Yes, it would,"
said Kass.
"There is nothing
I would love more
than to be your wife.
At last I can get away
from my father,
who hates me.
We will begin
our own life!"

"I want a big wedding!"
said Edward.

"How can we?"
Kass asked.
"My father won't give me
a big wedding."

"How do you know
until you ask him?"
Edward said.

"All right,"
said Kass.
"I will speak to him tonight."

"Better yet,"
said Edward,
"I will ask him
for your hand.
You will never be happy
until things are right
with your father."

Thinking It Over

1. What do you think
   Stan will do
   when Kass asks him
   to give her a wedding?

2. What kinds of things
   bring people together?

3. Did you ever know someone
   who wanted to get married
   just to get away from parents?

4. Do you believe that a man
   should ask a woman's father
   for her hand in marriage?

10 A Change of Heart

"Papa, Edward wants
to ask you something,"
Kass began. .

"Mr. Koloski,
I would like to marry
your daughter, Kass,"
said Edward.
"We would like
to have your blessing."

"I am surprised
to hear you ask this,"
said Stan.
"I didn't think
you two cared about
what I had to say."

"Your blessing
would mean a great deal,"
said Edward.

"We would like to have
a big wedding,
just like in Poland,"
added Kass.

"Is that so?"
said Stan.
He began to smile
as a picture came
into his head.
He saw himself and Kassia
dancing the polka
at her wedding.
"You have my blessing,"
he said.
"And nothing
would please me more
than to give my oldest daughter
a real Polish wedding!"

"Then it's all set,"
said Edward.
"We will get married
in your church.
The wedding Mass
will be said in Polish.

Then we will dance
at Dom Polski!"

Stan shook Edward's hand.
"You are more Polish
than I believed you were,"
Stan said.
"I am happy for you
to become my new son."

Then Stan turned
to his daughter.
"You are once again
a member of my family."

Kass was happy
for her father's change of heart.
She looked toward heaven.
Then she made
the sign of the cross.

Thinking It Over

1. Why do you think
   Kass and Edward
   want to have
   "a real Polish wedding"?

2. Why do you think
   Stan had a change of heart?

3. What is something
   that your parents
   would like to see you do?

11 A Real Polish Wedding

By this time,
Edward, Kass, and her family
knew many people.
It seemed as if
all the Poles in Buffalo
were in the church
on the wedding day.

Gregor was not yet
a full priest.
However, the church
let him stand up
with the parish priest
to marry Kass and Edward.

After the Mass,
everyone walked over
to Dom Polski.
A little polka band

played on the stage.
Everyone found someone
to dance with.
They danced the polka
in a big circle
around the room.
Many people wore
the bright-colored clothes
of the Fatherland.
It looked like
a real Polish wedding.

Then Stan stood up
in front of the crowd.
He waved his hands
for the band to stop.
"It is time
for the money dance!"
he shouted.
"If you wish to dance
with the bride or groom,
get out your money!
My other daughter
is ready with the white bag!

And now,
I shall have
the first dance
with my beautiful daughter!"

Stan put a dollar
into the white bag.
Then he took Kass's hand
and led her
onto the dance floor.
Father and daughter
began to polka
across the room.
Everyone stood at the edges
and watched
their happy faces.

"I dreamed a long time
of this day,"
said Stan.
"Here I am,
dancing the polka
with my daughter.
I dreamed of you
in a bright-colored dress.
But seeing you

in your wedding dress
is even better!"

  "This is the happiest day
of my life,"
said Kass.
"I love you, Papa.
And, Papa, please know this.
I am a Polish-American.
I am happy
to be an American.
But I will never forget
that I am the daughter of Poles.
I can never leave
the Polish part of me behind.
Just, please, Papa,
let me live
the American part of me."

  "You are
a married woman now,"
said Stan.
"You do as you please.
Just never forget
that Polish part of yourself.
It is important

to always remember
where you came from."

"I will always remember,"
said Kass.
She put both her arms
around her father
as they danced.

Then Zofia put a dollar
in the money bag.
She grabbed Edward's hand,
and the two of them
danced along with Stan and Kass.

In a few minutes,
there was a long line
of people waiting to dance
with Kass and Edward.
The money bag
became fat and heavy.
It held the down payment
on Kass's and Edward's
new home.

But it was four years
before they could move
out of the city.
Until then,
they would live
with Stan and Zofia
and the children.

Thinking It Over

1. What are weddings like in your family?

2. How would it work out if the married children lived with their parents in your family?

3. Do you believe it is important to always remember where you came from"?

12 Dancing the Polka

The second world war
began in 1939
when Germany
went into Poland.
"Why can't they
leave the Fatherland alone?"
Stan said
in front of his Polish club.

Stan and Zofia
had a telephone now.
Zofia got on the phone
to call Kass.
"A party is being held
at Dom Polski,"
she began.
"The money we raise
will help the new Poles
who come to the United States.

Why don't you and Edward
bring your children?"

"As a matter of fact,
Edward is very interested
in helping out,"
said Kass.
"But, Mama, you know
we're not much interested
in these Polish parties."

"It will be fun,"
said Zofia.
"Let your children
see our Polish dances.
Don't forget
what you told your father
at your wedding.
You told him
you would always remember
where you came from."

"So I did," said Kass.
"When is the dance?
We will all be there."

Kass looked around
the place she lived.
It was a nice house.
It sat by itself,
not part of a long row.
There was grass
in the front.
There was a driveway
for the car.
It wasn't like Poland.
And it wasn't like
Buffalo's East Side.
It was American.

Kass and Edward's children
spoke no Polish.
They made fun
of the bits of Polish
left in their parents' voices.
The family went to church,
but not a Polish church.
The children had never seen
anyone dance the polka.
All they knew of Poland
was the name of the country.

They were, after all,
American children.

The whole family
got into their car
and drove into Buffalo
to the Polish East Side.
"I haven't been
inside Dom Polski
for so many years,"
said Kass to Edward
at the front door.

They went inside
and up to the third floor.
The party was going strong.
There was the polka band,
up on the stage.
There were little rides
for the small children.
There was a long line
of people waiting
to buy *pirogies,*
the Polish potato dumplings.
People danced the polka
and other Polish folk dances.

And dancing right toward Kass
and her family
were Stan and Zofia Koloski.

Zofia wore a white blouse.
It had puffy sleeves.
Over the blouse
was a black vest,
cross-laced up the front.
Over her full, red skirt
Zofia had sewn
bright-colored flowers.

She spotted Kass's children.
She didn't stop dancing.
She just put out her hand
and pulled Kass's son
into the dance.
Stan grabbed the hand
of one of Kass's daughters.

"Look! There's Gregor!"
Kass shouted over the noise.

Gregor waved hello.
Then he grabbed

Kass's other daughter
and danced off with her.

Kass was surprised
to see her children
dance right along
with Stan, Zofia, and Gregor.
Edward laughed
to see the children
join right in
on the dance floor.

"Want to dance?"
he asked Kass.

"I feel out of place,"
she said.

"So what?"
said Edward.

With that,
the two of them
joined the polka dance.

"Edward, this is fun!"
laughed Kass.
"I told my father
I would always remember
where I came from.
There's nothing like the polka
to help a person
remember she's Polish!"

Kass never did forget.
And because she and Edward
took their family
to the party that day,
her children never forgot either.

Thinking It Over

1. What kinds of things
   help you remember
   where you came from?

2. How important is it
   to pass along old ideas
   to your children?

3. What ties to the past
   do you think
   are most important?
   Why?